PUFFIN BOOKS

Published by the Penguin Group
Penguin Books Ltd, 80 Strand, London WC2R 0RL, England
Penguin Group (USA), Inc., 375 Hudson Street, New York, New York 10014, USA
Penguin Books Australia Ltd, 250 Camberwell Road, Camberwell, Victoria 3124, Australia
Penguin Books Canada Ltd, 10 Alcorn Avenue, Toronto, Ontario, Canada M4V 3B2
Penguin Books India (P) Ltd, 11 Community Centre, Panchsheel Park, New Delhi – 110 017, India
Penguin Books (NZ) Ltd, Cnr Rosedale and Airborne Roads, Albany, Auckland, New Zealand
Penguin Books (South Africa) (Pty) Ltd, 24 Sturdee Avenue, Rosebank 2196, South Africa

Penguin Books Ltd, Registered Offices: 80 Strand, London WC2R 0RL, England

www.penguin.com

First published by Levinson's Children's Books in hardback in 1997
First published by Gullane Children's Books in paperback in 2002
First published in Puffin Books 2004
5 7 9 10 8 6 4

Text copyright © Ian Whybrow, 1997
Illustrations copyright © Adrian Reynolds, 1997
All rights reserved

The moral right of the author and illustrator has been asserted

Manufactured in China

British Library Cataloguing in Publication Data
A CIP catalogue record for this book is available from the British Library

ISBN-13: 978-0-14056-986-5
ISBN-10: 0-14056-986-3

This

Harry

book belongs to

....

Harry
and the
Snow
King

Ian Whybrow and Adrian Reynolds

PUFFIN

When the snow came, you had to look for it.
But Harry had waited long enough.
He went out with his spoon and plate.

He put out his tongue and caught a flake.
It was just right.

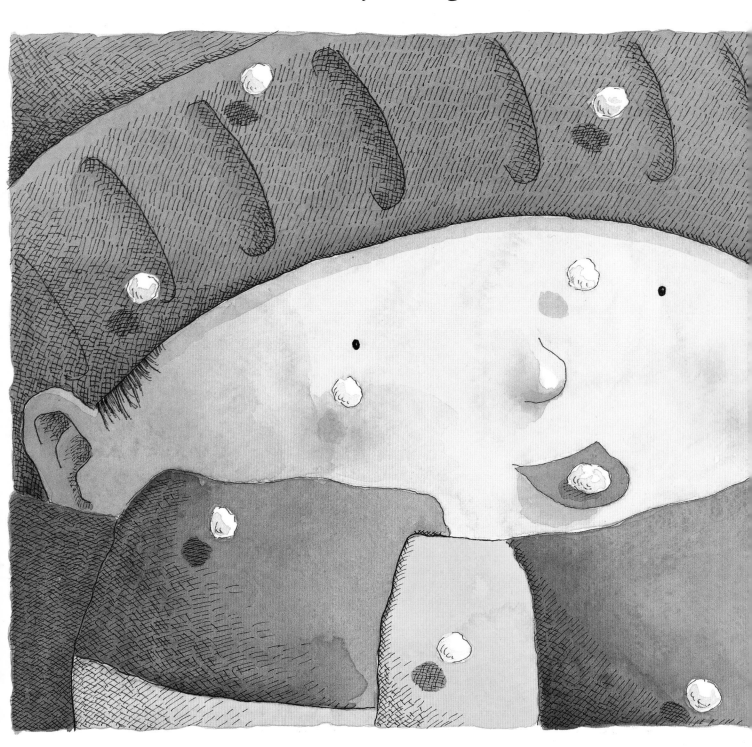

There was some in the corner by the woodpile.
There was a good bit by the henhouse.

And if you were very careful
you could scoop it off the leaves.

It took all morning to find enough snow
to make the snow king.

Nan called, "What are you doing out there?"
"Nothing," he said. But he was looking
on the holly for red buttons.

Mum called, "Are you hungry?"
"Not yet," he said.
He was hungry, but he was making a crown.

Sam said, "Your soup is cold, stupid."
"Coming," he said, and brought the
snow king to show them.

They all bowed down to look.

Sam said not to bring him in,
it was too warm inside.

That was why Harry left
the snow king on the wall.

He ate his soup and told about the snow king.

Sam said big snowmen were better and he was stupid not to have waited.

That was why Harry threw his bread at Sam.

Nan took him to his room
to settle down.

Later, the snow king was not on the wall.

"You just give him back!" Harry said.
But Sam had been watching TV all the time.

The snow king was
nowhere in the yard.
He was not in the refrigerator.

"Somebody kidnapped him," said Harry.

He wanted to call the police
but Mum said better not to bother them.

Four o'clock, Mr Oakley passed
on his tractor. Harry said
about his snow king
being kidnapped.

Mr Oakley looked up at the sky.
He said not to give up hope.
He said maybe the snow king
went to order more snow.

Next morning there were
snowpeople all over the yard.

Ten at least. Wonderful!
And white everywhere, everywhere you looked!

Mr Oakley drove by on his way back from milking. "I found these earlier," he said. He opened his hand to show the red buttons and the crown.

"I hoped all night," said Harry.
"I never gave up. It was just like you said.
The snow king went to order some more snow,
but he left me these snowpeople."

"Hitch up your sledge," said Mr Oakley.
"This looks like good snow for getting towed
by a tractor. Shall we go now, or wait for Sam?"

"Sam's watching TV," said Harry.

"We'll come back for her later then,"
said Mr Oakley. "You get first go."

Harry and Sam had a lot of fun that day.
But, that first go was just the best.

Look out for all of Harry's adventures!

ISBN 0140569804

Harry and the Bucketful of Dinosaurs

Harry finds some old, plastic dinosaurs and cleans them, finds out their names and takes them everywhere with him – until, one day, they get lost … Will he ever find them?

Harry and the Snow King

There's just enough snow for Harry to build a very small snow king. But then the snow king disappears – who's kidnapped him?

ISBN 0140569863

ISBN 0140569820

Harry and the Robots

Harry's robot is sent to the toy hospital to be fixed, so Harry and Nan decide to make a new one. When Nan has to go to hospital, Harry knows just how to help her get better!

Harry and the Dinosaurs say "Raahh!"

Harry's dinosaurs are acting strangely. They're hiding all over the house, refusing to come out … Could it be because today is the day of Harry's dentist appointment?

ISBN 0140569812

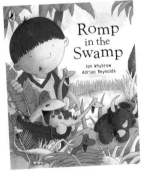

ISBN 0140569847

Harry and the Dinosaurs Romp in the Swamp

Harry has to play at Charlie's house and doesn't want to share his dinosaurs. But when Charlie builds a fantastic swamp, Harry and the dinosaurs can't help but join in the fun!

Harry and the Dinosaurs make a Christmas Wish

Harry and the dinosaurs would *love* to own a duckling. They wait till Christmas and make a special wish, but Santa leaves them something even more exciting…!

ISBN 0141380179 (hbk)
ISBN 0140569529 (pbk)

ISBN 0140569839

ISBN 0140569855

Harry and the Dinosaurs play Hide-and-Seek
Harry and the Dinosaurs have a Very Busy Day

Join in with Harry and his dinosaurs for some peep-through fold-out fun! These exciting books about shapes and colours make learning easy!